JE

04323723°

CH

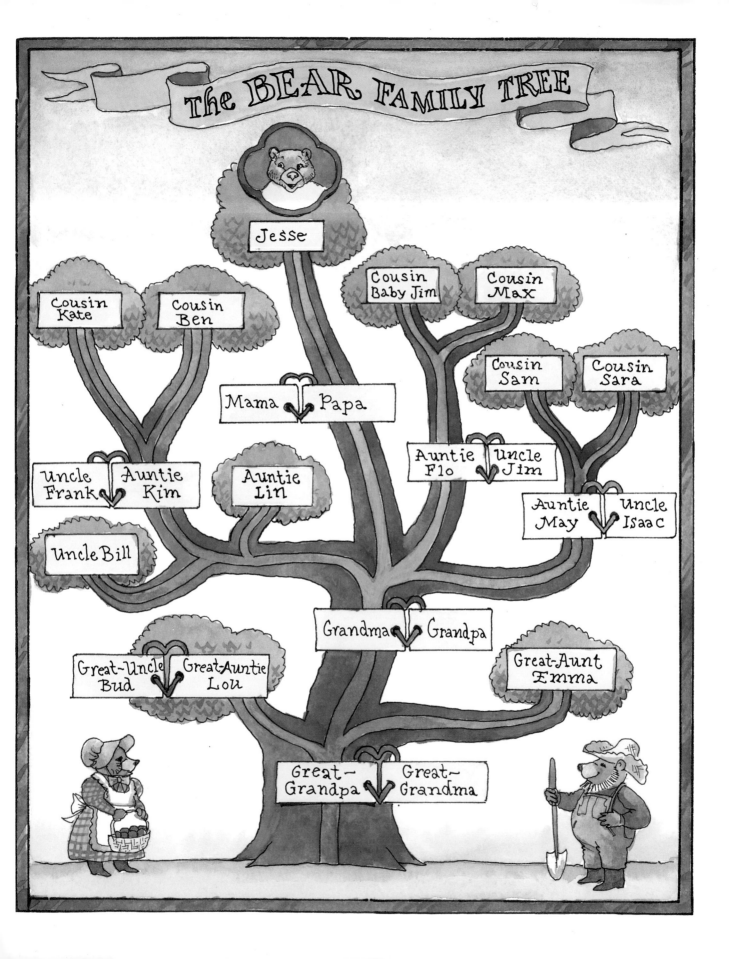

Climb the Family Tree, Jesse Bear!

by **Nancy White Carlstrom**

illustrated by **Bruce Degen**

Simon & Schuster Books for Young Readers

New York London Toronto Sydney

OTHER BOOKS IN THE JESSE BEAR SERIES

BY NANCY WHITE CARLSTROM,

ILLUSTRATED BY BRUCE DEGEN

Better Not Get Wet, Jesse Bear
Guess Who's Coming, Jesse Bear
Happy Birthday, Jesse Bear!
How Do You Say It Today, Jesse Bear?
It's About Time, Jesse Bear
Jesse Bear, What Will You Wear?
Let's Count It Out, Jesse Bear
What a Scare, Jesse Bear
Where Is Christmas, Jesse Bear?

SIMON & SCHUSTER BOOKS FOR YOUNG READERS
An imprint of Simon & Schuster Children's Publishing Division
1230 Avenue of the Americas, New York, New York 10020

Book design by Greg Stadnyk
The text of this book is set in 18-point Goudy Bold.
The illustrations are rendered in pen and ink and watercolor.
Manufactured in China
2 4 6 8 10 9 7 5 3 1
Library of Congress Cataloging-in-Publication Data
Carlstrom, Nancy White.
Climb the family tree, Jesse Bear! / by Nancy White Carlstrom ; illustrated by Bruce Degen.—1st ed.
p. cm.
Summary: Jesse Bear experiences the excitement of a family reunion filled with grandparents, aunts, uncles, and cousins and lots of food, games, and storytelling.
ISBN 0-689-80701-5
[1. Family reunions—Fiction. 2. Bears—Fiction. 3. Stories in rhyme.] I. Degen, Bruce, ill. II. Title.
PZ8.3.C21684 Cl 2002
[E]—dc21   2001020579

For my family past, present, and future
—N. W. C.

For Eliezer and Hannah,
who replanted the Degen family tree
on this happy shore.
—B. D.

Are we there yet? Are we there yet?

We're here, Jesse Bear! We're here!

There's Grandpa in his funny hat
And Grandma by the well.
We'll help them pick the strawberries
And put them out to sell.

My favorite, Uncle Bill, is here.
He flew in his new plane.
Maybe he'll take me up with him,
Unless there's wind or rain.

Auntie Lin and Auntie Kim
And old Great-Auntie Lou
Wear their shawls and pat my head
And say, "Oh, look at you!"

The cousins are in every size.
The baby's in my chair.
When I get too close to him,
He always pulls my hair.

There's Great-Grandpa's photo
At the end of the long hall,
And Great-Grandmother's quilt
Is hanging on the wall.

Great-Aunt Emma's paintings
And Cousin Ben's smooth stones,
Small boxes and birdhouses
And prehistoric bones!

We hear family tales of long ago:
Weddings by the tree,
The day you raced to the hospital,
The day you first saw me!

The fireflies light the evening.
There's a very starry sky.
The younger aunts do a dance,
The older aunts all sigh.

Grandpa plays his old fiddle
And tells where it came from.
Auntie May strums away
While all the cousins hum.

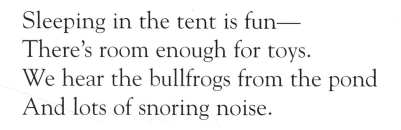

Sleeping in the tent is fun—
There's room enough for toys.
We hear the bullfrogs from the pond
And lots of snoring noise.

The next day we go boating

And take a long hayride.

Aunts and uncles play croquet. The cousins run and hide.

There's laughing and there's crying

And sometimes even fights,

But we always find a way
Of making wrong things right.

The uncles talk of all the things
They like to do the best.
The aunts tell stories one by one,
And Grandpa takes a rest.

We smell flowers from the garden,
Grass that's had a trim,
Grandma's bread and apple pie,
Sweet rolls by Uncle Jim.

We taste Aunt Flo's cherry jam
And berries from the vine.
Ice cream we make and eat with cake
Will taste especially fine.

It feels so good to see them all—
Our family in one spot.
Some are different, some the same.
Some like to hug a lot!

Grandma has the trunk brought out
Of faded family clothes.
The cousins all dress up in them
And for the pictures pose.

But the most exciting thing
That's special, just for me—
This is the year I'm old enough
To climb the family tree!